Time Out

by Bobbi JG Weiss & David Cody Weiss

Illustrated by Victoria Miller

SCHOLASTIC INC.

New York Toronto London Auckland Sydney
Mexico City New Delhi Hong Kong Buenos Aires

No part of this publication may be reproduced in whole or in part,
or stored in a retrieval system, or transmitted in any form or
by any means, electronic, mechanical, photocopying, recording,
or otherwise, without written permission of the publisher.

Published by Scholastic Inc.,
90 Old Sherman Turnpike, Danbury, Connecticut 06816.

SCHOLASTIC and associated logos are trademarks
and/or registered trademarks of Scholastic Inc.

ISBN 0-439-56280-5

First Scholastic Printing, January 2004

Chapters

BLAM! The front door burst open. "Home at last!" cried Timmy Turner, flopping onto the couch and flipping through the new issue of *T.V. Today.* "I can't wait to watch 'America's Funniest Dental Exams'!"

"Only if you're on schedule, young man," his mother added.

Timmy shuddered. He knew what the daily "schedule" was, all right. "But Mom, it's educational!" he cried, defending his favorite TV show.

"Now, Timmy, you know the drill," said his father, agreeing with his wife. "First

TV
TODAY

there's homework time, then chore time, then dinnertime, then clean-up time, and *then* there's TV time."

"Yeah, I know, I know," said Timmy. "But don't you think it's time I got a time out from all those other things?"

Timmy's mother and father left the room laughing.

"Oh, Timmy, you have such an

imagination!" Mrs. Turner said over her shoulder. "You can't just call a 'time out' anytime you want it to be a different time!"

Timmy just grinned. "What a great idea!" he thought.

Chapter 2
A Timely Wish

Timmy called for his fairy godparents,
who appeared in a poof of magic dust.

"Hi, Timmy!" Wanda greeted him.
"What's up?"

"Ooo, look at his face, look at his face!" cried Cosmo. "He's got that I'm-going-to-make-a-really-freaky-wish look!"

"Yup!" Timmy said. "I'm tired of a schedule running my life. I always have to wait for *later* to do what I want to do *now*."

"But, Timmy, that's the way the world works," explained Wanda. "Time keeps order throughout the universe."

"It sure does!" Cosmo agreed. "Why, without time, there would be no time like the present! Except maybe for the past, which *was* the present a few minutes ago . . . "

"The point is, Timmy, schedules have a purpose," Wanda said.

"Well, I'm sick of them!" said Timmy. "I wish there were no scheduled times for anything anymore! Then it would be any *time* I say it is—"

"—and I say it's *permanent playtime!*"

Timmy hurried outside. "Man, this is gonna be great! I won't have to do homework or chores or clean up ever again! I can just play until my favorite show is on TV!"

Chester and A.J. met him on the sidewalk.

"Hey, Timmy," said A.J., "it's playtime!"

"Yeah, dude!" said Chester. "What do you want to play?"

"What else?" Timmy replied. "Timmy Ball!"

"AAAAAGH!" cried Chester and A.J.,
scattering as Timmy lobbed the ball at them.

The ball smacked A.J. in the rear. "YOWCH!" he yelled. Then he added thoughtfully, "You know, despite the pain involved in playing Timmy Ball, I find it gratifying to see everyone in the neighborhood enjoying themselves as much as we are."

"Yeah—OOOF!" Chester said as the next ball bounced off his head and he looked around. "Who'd have thought that *playing* would bring the whole world together in universal peace and harmony?"

25

An hour later, Timmy was exhausted.
"Wow, I haven't had so
much fun since . . . well,
since the last time I had
so much fun!" he thought.
"I need a break."

Chapter 4
Time to Say
OOPS!

Timmy went to the kitchen for a snack and found his parents looking through the cupboards.

"Your father lost his marbles," his mother explained.

"Can't play marbles without marbles!" his father added. "Don't worry, I'll find them!"

Timmy's stomach was growling, so he reached for a cookie.

"Timmy, it's not snack time," his mother scolded him. "It's playtime, remember?"

"But I'm hungry," said Timmy. "When is dinnertime?"

"What's dinnertime?" his mother asked.

A horrible thought struck Timmy. He checked the pot on the stove. It was *empty!* "You're not cooking anything!" he cried.

"Well, of course not," she replied.

"I found them!" said Timmy's father, pulling a bag of marbles out of a cereal box.

To Timmy's shock, his parents started
to play marbles right there on the floor.
"Mom!" he cried. "Dad! Aren't we going
to eat?"

"It's not time to eat!" his parents
chorused. "It's time to play!"

31

Chapter 5
Freak-out Time!

Timmy ran through the house, checking
all the clocks. To his dismay, all the clock
hands were spinning wildly.

Outside the full moon was high in the
sky along with the sun. Even the stars were
out—in the *daytime!*

"What have I done?" Timmy moaned.
"Instead of creating nonstop fun time, I've
erased time altogether!"

"There's no more dinnertime or lunchtime or breakfast time— not even snack time!

Everybody will starve!"

"With no bedtime, nobody will ever be able to *sleep!* Without down time, I'll never be able to sit and pointlessly stare at *nothing* for hours on end!"

"And without TV time, I can't watch 'America's Funniest Dental Exams'—despite the fact that it's educational!"

Timmy realized there was only one way to fix things. "Cosmo!" he called. "Wanda! *Hel-l-l-l-lp!*"

Timmy quickly told his fairy godparents
how his wish had gone completely wonky.
"You have to let me un-wish it," he said.

"Can't," said Cosmo flatly. "It's playtime!"

"Rummy!" shouted Wanda. "I win!"

"Look, if I make a wish, you have to grant it," Timmy insisted.

"No, dear!" Wanda told him. "Granting wishes is our job, and it's not work time!"

"It's playtime!" Cosmo said again.

Timmy thought hard. "How can I make them grant me a wish? All they want to do is play games!" And then he had an idea.

"Hey!" he said, "Why don't we play 'Let's Make a Wish!'"

Chapter 6
Game Time!

Cosmo and Wanda loved game shows.
POOF! Timmy found himself
on a game show set.

42

"Ladies and gentlemen!" came Cosmo's voice over the speakers. "Welcome to 'Let's Make a Wish!'—the game where Timmy Turner can win *one wish* if he answers all the questions correctly!"

"Our first category is—Skunks!" said Cosmo. "The question: How do you keep a skunk from smelling?"

Timmy didn't even have to think about it.

He hit his buzzer. "Hold its nose?"

Timmy answered.

Ding-ding-ding! rang a loud bell.
Confetti fell, Wanda clapped, and Timmy
grinned. "That was easy!" he thought.

DING!
DING!
DING!

"Our second category is—Keys!"
announced Cosmo. "The question: If a door
key opens a door, and a mailbox key opens
a mailbox, what does a monkey open?"

"Bananas!" Timmy answered.

Ding-ding-ding! rang the bell. Fireworks went off, Wanda clapped, and Timmy grinned again. "I'll win that wish in no time!" he thought.

"Our third and final category is—Really Painful Things!" said Cosmo. "The question: What do you call the procedure where the nerve of a heavily decayed tooth is removed and replaced with a filling material?"

Timmy froze. "But—but that's a hard one!" he thought in surprise. "I don't know the answer!"

"Uh . . . " he muttered as he tried to think quickly. "Uhhh . . . "

Suddenly Timmy remembered his favorite episode of 'America's Funniest Dental Exams.' "A root canal!" he shouted out, hitting his buzzer. "The answer is a root canal!"

"Timmy Turner, you are correct!" declared

Cosmo. "You WIN!"

"But, Timmy, how did you know the answer to such a difficult question?" asked Wanda.

"I watch TV!" Timmy said. "It's educational!"

"Who'd have thought?" said Cosmo. "Now make your wish!"

53

"I wish time was back to normal!" exclaimed Timmy.

Cosmo and Wanda pointed their wands. "You've got it, sport!" they said together.

Chapter 7
Time to Finish This Story

Timmy was instantly back home.

Everything was normal again.

"Congratulations, Timmy!" said Wanda.

"It was about *TIME*, too!" said Cosmo.

Timmy glanced at his watch. "And

speaking of time—"

"—it's time to watch 'America's Funniest Dental Exams'!"

"But, Timmy," said Wanda, "don't you have homework time, chore time, dinnertime, and clean-up time before TV time?"

"Not this time!" said Timmy. "I wish that I could fast forward through all those other times and go right to TV time!"

Timmy got his wish, all right. Suddenly
the entire neighborhood was in front
of the TV.

"Oh no," he groaned. "I'm going
to have to fix this all over again!"
Then he sat down, adding, "Just
as soon as my
favorite show
is over."